Some Days Are Lonely

Written by Yeong-ah Kim
Illustrated by Ji-soo Shin
Edited by Joy Cowley

big & SMALL

No matter how hard I look,
there is no one near.
I call out in a loud voice,
but there is no answer.
I feel there is only me
in the whole world.

3

Squish, squish! Squish, squish!
My feet sink into the mud.
My heart feels heavy.

6

Dark clouds fill the sky.
That's how I feel.
All my thoughts
are like dark clouds
dropping a rain of tears.

I sit by the pond,
all by myself.
Some days are lonely.

Some days I sigh all the time.
Some days I wish the ground
would open up and swallow me.

I feel that the sun shines
on the rest of the world,
but not on me.
There is a cold wind
blowing right through me.

I don't know why
I am so sad.
I cry and cry.

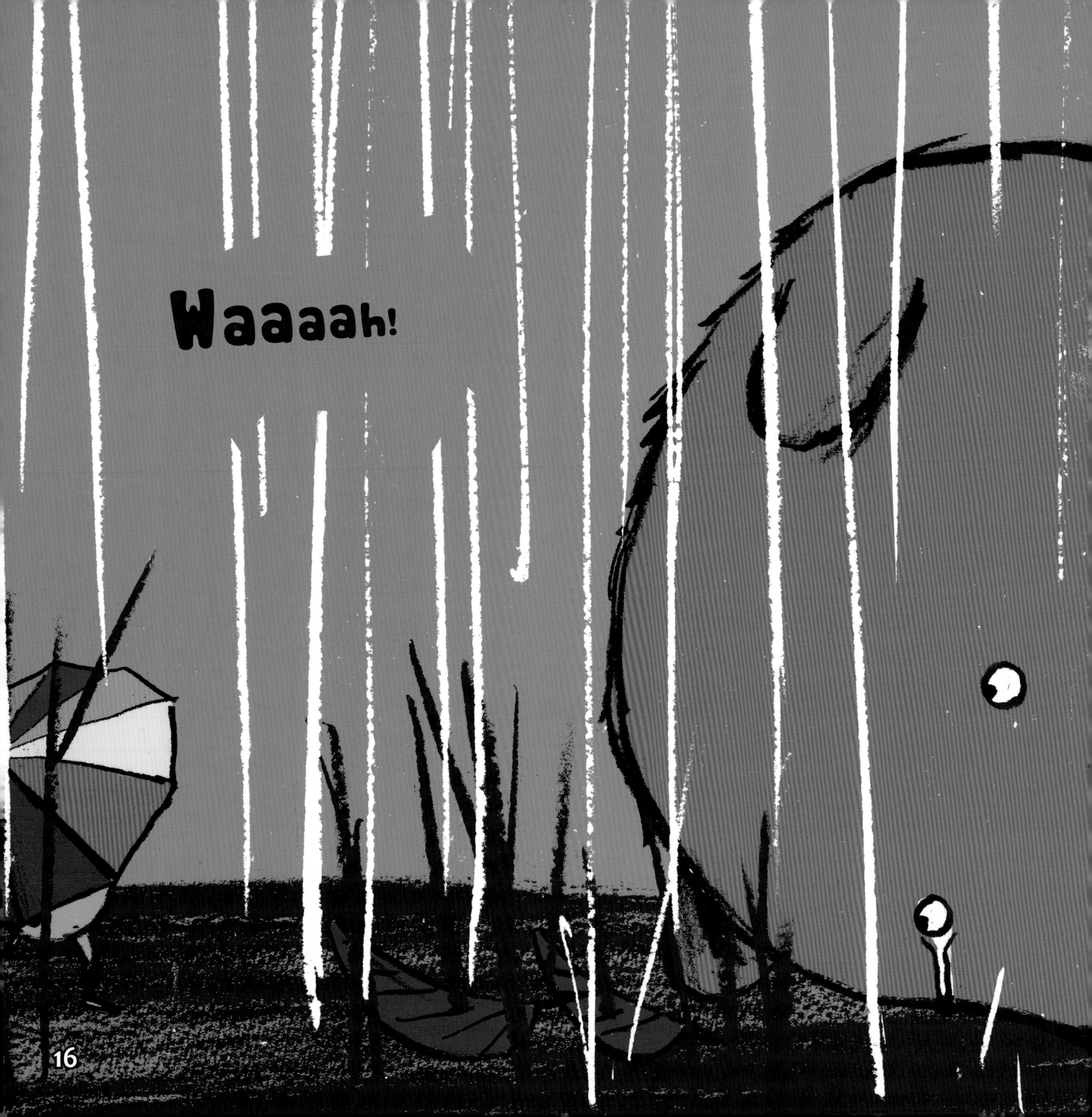
Waaaah!

17

But wait!

Nothing stays the same.

Things change.

The rain stops.

The clouds go away,

and a friend comes.

Splash!

Everyone has lonely days.
Lonely days are like storms,
but the sun always comes out.

It is rain and sun together

that makes rainbows.

Little Bear,

Today you looked tired and sad.

You felt very lonely.

Don't worry, little Bear.

Everyone gets lonely.

But loneliness passes.

When you feel that way,

talk to your friends or your family.

Read a book. Listen to music.

When the rain of loneliness stops,

you may see a real rainbow

in your heart.

From your friend,

Frog

big & SMALL

Original Korean text by Yeong-ah Kim

Illustrations by Ji-soo Shin

Original Korean edition © EenBook

This English edition published by Big & Small in 2015
by arrangement with EenBook

English text edited by Joy Cowley

Additional editing by Mary Lindeen

Artwork for this edition produced
in cooperation with Norwood House Press, USA

English edition © Big & Small 2015

ISBN: 978-1-925233-96-4

Printed in Korea